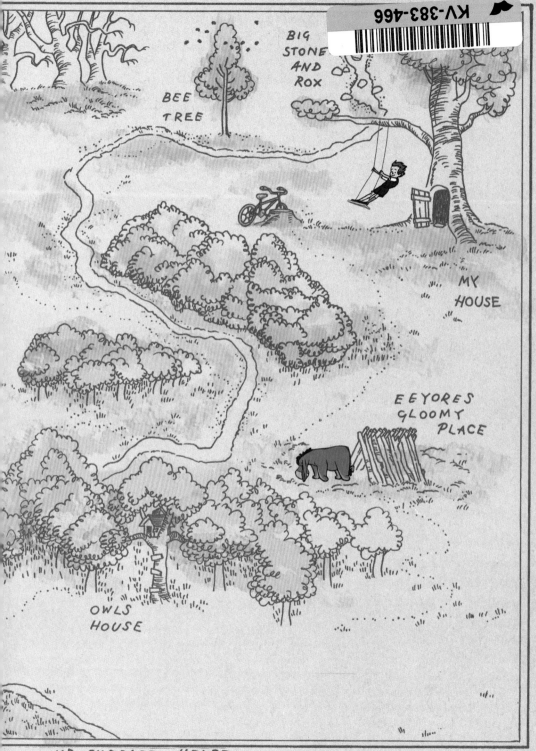

© 2018 Disney Enterprises, Inc.
Based on the "Winnie the Pooh" works, by A.A. Milne and E.H. Shepard.
Published by Hachette Partworks Ltd.
ISBN: 978-1-910360-20-0
Date of Printing: June 2018
Printed in Romania by Canale

Deep in the Hundred-Acre Wood lived a boy named Christopher Robin and his stuffed bear, Winnie the Pooh.

One morning, Pooh woke up with a very rumbly tummy. He needed honey! But Pooh didn't have any honey at home, so he went outside to find some.

First, Pooh went to Eeyore's house. But Eeyore didn't have any honey. Pooh noticed that Eeyore also didn't have a tail.

"I, Winnie the Pooh, will find you a tail," he announced. "And after that, I shall get some honey."

Just then, a voice came
from a nearby tree.

It was Owl. He was reading
out stories he had written about
his life.

Pooh and Eeyore told him about
Eeyore's missing tail.

Owl came up with an idea.
"We'll make a sign, promising a
reward to anyone who finds a tail for
Eeyore," Owl declared.

The friends went to ask Christopher Robin to help them make a notice. He suggested a competition to find Eeyore a new tail. The winner would get a special prize – a pot of honey.

Everyone came up with all kinds of new tails for Eeyore. But none of them worked quite as well as his old one.

Finally, Eeyore tried a scarf that Kanga had
knitted. He really liked it, so Kanga won the prize.
But sadly, the new tail didn't last. Before long,
the wool unravelled and Eeyore was tailless again.

Later, Pooh went to Christopher Robin's house in search of honey. He didn't find any, but he did spot a note on the doorstep.

The note said, *'Gone out, busy Backson. Signed, Christopher Robin.'*

Pooh showed the note to Owl. "Christopher Robin has been captured by a creature called the Backson!" decided Owl.

"What's a Backson?" asked Roo.

Owl drew a monster with shaggy fur. He explained that the Backson was a thoughtless creature that scribbled in books, spoiled milk and put holes in socks.

Rabbit came up with a plan. They would lure the Backson to a big hole, then trap the monster in the hole and refuse to let him out until he let Christopher Robin go.

They needed to lay a trail, so everyone started
collecting things that the Backson would like,
while Pooh and Piglet set off to dig the hole. Pooh
supervised while Piglet dug and dug.

Piglet and Pooh covered the pit with a cloth
and put an empty honeypot on it, to make the
trap look like a picnic.

But Tigger wanted to capture the Backson his way. "Come on, Eeyore! You and me are going to catch that Backson together," he cried. "Let's get you Tiggerised!"

First, Tigger painted stripes on Eeyore, then he dressed up as a Backson, so he could teach Eeyore how to catch him. Poor Eeyore. Being Tiggerish really wasn't his strong point.

Suddenly, Tigger lost sight of Eeyore. Had the Backson struck again and taken his friend? He searched everywhere, not realising that Eeyore was hiding – from Tigger!

In the woods, Pooh spotted the pot of honey on the picnic blanket, and completely forgot that it was a trap! His friends found poor Pooh at the bottom of the hole, with the empty pot on his head.

Just then, Eeyore arrived wearing an anchor as a tail. Rabbit threw the anchor into the pit to rescue Pooh, but somehow all the friends fell in with it... except Piglet.

Piglet went to find something to help him free his friends. Soon, he found his friend, B'loon.

Just then, a huge shadow appeared. It was Tigger dressed as the Backson, but Piglet didn't notice the Tigger part.

"B-B-B-BACKSON!" Piglet shouted. He grabbed B'loon and ran for his life, with Tigger chasing after them.

Down they both tumbled into the hole, as B'loon floated off.

Tigger had dropped his honeypot shoe on the edge of the hole.

Pooh was still hungry. He looked around and spotted some letters, so he made them into a ladder and climbed up to the pot – but it was empty.

Then Rabbit noticed the letter ladder. "We can get out!" he cried.

The friends climbed out of the pit just as Christopher Robin and B'loon arrived.

"How did you escape the Backson?" Rabbit asked.

"What on *earth* is a Backson?" said Christopher Robin, puzzled.

Owl explained and Pooh showed Christopher Robin the note. Christopher Robin laughed. He explained that he'd written, "Back soon", not "Backson".

It was all a silly misunderstanding!

Since it was rather late, Christopher Robin suggested they all go home. But first, Rabbit gave B'loon a honeypot prize for finding Christopher Robin and bringing him to the pit.

Pooh's tummy was still very rumbly. He
remembered there was honey at Owl's house, so
he went there and pulled Owl's new bell rope. He
stared at the bell rope for a moment, thinking that
it looked familiar.

Owl invited Pooh in and began to tell him about the new bell rope he had found hanging over a thistle bush.

"That's Eeyore's tail!" cried Pooh. He had to get the tail back to Eeyore right away – so he and his tummy left without even a taste of Owl's honey.

Christopher Robin decided that for finding
Eeyore's proper tail, and for thinking of his friend
instead of his rumbly tummy, Pooh deserved the
biggest and best prize of all.

And that's how Pooh ended up inside an
absolutely *enormous* pot of honey!

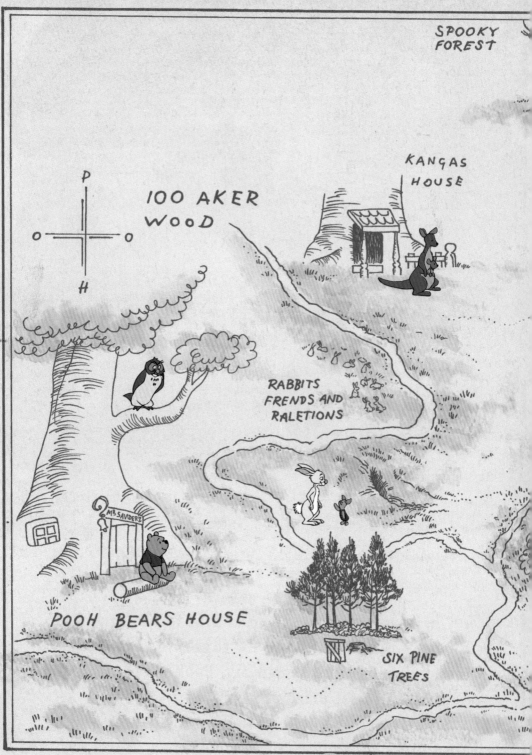

SPOOKY FOREST

100 AKER WOOD

KANGAS HOUSE

RABBITS FRENDS AND RALETIONS

MR SANDERZ

POOH BEARS HOUSE

SIX PINE TREES

DRAWN BY ME AND